W9-DCD-540

TOUGH GUY

Text by Bianca Bradbury

Illustrated by Marie C. Nichols

HOUGHTON MIFFLIN COMPANY BOSTON
The Riverside Press, Cambridge
1953

F

Tough Guy sat in the window of his apartment, twitching his tail.

He didn't look like a tough guy. He was a Persian kitten with round blue eyes, and he was just as soft and fluffy as a powder puff.

He twitched his tail, sitting there in the window, because he knew he looked like a sissy, and in his heart he was a real tough cat.

How could he ever prove it, if he had to stay cooped up all day? How could he get out? The door was in his way.

He wanted to get out, to feel the ground under his feet. He could see the ground from his window. The window was on the top floor. The sky was right over his head. There was a brick wall, just like his, across a narrow alley. If he twisted his neck around the corner, he could see trees, and a piece of grass.

A ledge, four inches wide, ran past outside his window. He thought about exploring it. Then he looked down, and right away he was dizzy. No, there was no way out.

He was thinking so hard about his troubles, he didn't see a cat jump into the window across the alley. Tough Guy looked up, and suddenly, there it was. Tough Guy jumped, and almost fell out. He arched his fluffy back and hissed. The other cat just stared.

He was small, too, and his coat was striped black and gray, with white patches. His nose, however, was pointed. Tough Guy was a Persian, so his nose was flat. Tough Guy thought to himself, That is the way a cat ought to look—thin and tough. Not soft and round.

The other cat yawned. "What's your name?" he asked.

"Tough Guy."

"You don't look like a tough guy. You look like a powder puff."

"Oh, is that so?" Tough Guy could think of nothing else to say.

The other cat stretched out on his window. He tucked his paws under him and went to sleep.

"I'm tougher than you are," Tough Guy said loudly.

"I'm TWICE as tough as you are."

The cat opened one green eye. "Go away, Powder Puff," he said. "Let me sleep." And he shut the eye.

Tough Guy was so angry, he swelled up into a ball. The striped cat just went on sleeping. Tough Guy, mad clear through, jumped down from his window, and hid under a chair and sulked.

The next morning, when he was alone in the apartment, he climbed up in his window. He waited for the striped cat to appear, and when it did, he was glad. After all, he did get lonesome, keeping house all by himself in the apartment during the daytime. "Hello," he called.

"Hi, Powder Puff," said the striped cat.

Tough Guy began to feel mad, but he stayed where he was, this time. "What's your name?" he asked.

"Joe."

Joe stretched himself and yawned. Then he began to show off. He stepped out of his window and walked along the ledge that ran outside his building. He came to the corner and turned and walked back. "Let's see you do that," he said.

Tough Guy looked along his ledge. He looked down. Right away, he felt dizzy in the head. "I don't feel like it today," he said.

"You're scared."

"I am not scared!"

"I bet you're even scared of a mouse," said Joe.

"I am not!"

"I bet you couldn't even smell one," said Joe. "You haven't any nose. Where's your nose?"

"I have too got a nose! It's flat because I'm a pedigreed Persian kitten."

Joe yawned right in his face. "You're a pedigreed Persian Powder Puff," Joe said, and jumped into his own house. Tough Guy was left alone to sulk.

I'll show him, he told himself. I'll show him!

That night, in his sleep, he lashed his fluffy tail, thinking of what Joe had said. The next morning, he was on the window sill bright and early. Joe appeared, said "Good morning," and stretched out, as usual, to sleep.

"What makes you so sleepy?" Tough Guy asked.

"I've been out on the roof all night," yawned Joe.

Tough Guy yawned too, a big, deep yawn. "I'm sleepy too," he said. "I was out on the roof all night, too."

"I can't believe it," Joe said.

"I was, too. I chased a mouse on the roof!"

"There aren't any mice on the roof," said Joe. "The mice are in the park. You have to go along the ledge and down the iron stairs. You cross the street, and there's the park and there's the mouse."

What made him say it, Tough Guy didn't know. The words popped out before he thought. "All right," he said. "If you know so much about the park and the mouse, show me."

Joe opened one eye and then the other, very surprised. "Do you mean it?"

"I mean it," Tough Guy said.

Joe got up, and marched off along the ledge. His striped black and gray tail waved like a banner. He disappeared around the corner.

Tough Guy was left alone. He had sounded very brave. Now he had to BE brave.

He eased himself out on the ledge. "I'll show that Joe," he growled. He started off. Down below, there was just a lot of air. The wind flattened him against the bricks, but paw after paw he crept along. At the corner it was dreadful. Underneath him was a noisy street with cars rushing and bells clanging and horns blowing. He shut his eyes and felt sick, very sick.

When he opened them, Joe was out of sight. Tough Guy knew he must either go back or go on. He went on.

Sure enough, he came to the iron stairs Joe had told about. Now the ledge part was over. But oh, dear. The stairs were just iron slats, nothing nice and solid. And they went down, and down, and down.

He tried going head first but that was bad, for he had to look down and that made him dizzy. So he tried going tail first. That was better. He hung on to one step with his front feet and felt for the next step with his back feet. That way, he crept down, stair by stair, with his eyes shut.

At last, he got up his courage and looked down. The ground wasn't far away. He turned himself around, and bounced down the last few stairs.

He found himself in an alley. It opened into a street, where traffic rushed by and people were hurrying on the sidewalk. Beyond, there lay the greenness of the park. Hugging the wall, and his heart pounding so it almost jumped out of his body, Tough Guy scampered through the alley.

The people paid no attention as he slid under their feet. The cars paid no attention either. He sat down on the curb. The street was a river of rushing cars. How did cats get across? How did Joe get across? Birds could do it easily. But cats didn't have wings.

Then, with a squeaking and grinding, the cars stopped. They were minding some kind of light that turned from green to red. Tough Guy picked up his fluffy feet and flew across.

The park was just beyond the fence. Tough Guy made himself small and squeezed under the fence. And there he was.

He looked about. There was Joe, curled like a leaf, nose on paws, watching him. "I see you made it," said Joe.

"Yes," said Tough Guy. He felt real tough, a real stout fellow.

"Let's get on to the business of the mouse," said Joe.

He led the way. They went along a grass path. Tough Guy marched proudly, tail high. They came to a thicket of bushes. "There's usually a mouse or two in here," Joe told him. "You go in one side, and I'll go in the other. There's a pond on the other side of the thicket, so if you start a mouse, you chase him my way. You don't know anything about mice. I'll have to show you how to catch him. You just chase him toward me."

Tough Guy, twitching his whiskers with excitement, poked his nose into the bushes. He could hear Joe creeping softly, and the dry leaves rustling. He inched along, trying to see ahead, listening for Joe, watching for a mouse.

Would he know one if he saw it? He had heard about mice and dreamed about mice. But when he came right down to it, he hadn't any idea what mice really were. So he kept a special sharp eye out.

Something gray and furry leaped up right in front of his nose. So that was a mouse! Tough Guy let out a yip and scrambled after. The mouse was fast but so was Tough Guy. They went crashing through the underbrush. "Chase him my way!" Joe yowled. "Chase him my way!"

But Tough Guy was too excited and too pleased with himself to listen. Why should he let Joe have the fun? It's my mouse, he thought. I've found it and I've chased it and I'll catch it!

The mouse was smart. It kept just out of Tough Guy's reach. It darted this way and that, circling around. It doubled back on its tracks, just a bit out of reach. Tough Guy was getting too tired to look where he was going. He bumped into branches and through the leaves. He never took his eyes away from the mouse.

Then, the mouse shot off in a new direction. Tough Guy was too mixed up to change his direction quickly. He rushed on. The bushes stopped. Beyond the bushes there was, suddenly, water.

He tried to put on his brakes but he couldn't. He shot off the bank, sailed through the air and landed, kerplunk, in the pond. The water closed over his head.

He went down, down, down.

It seemed to him like hours that he struggled to get to the top of the water. Then out his head popped and he breathed the good air. He thrashed with his feet and scrabbled to shore and scrambled up the bank.

He looked a mess. Every fluffy hair was plastered flat with water and mud. His lovely tail was a wet, dirty string. He sat on the bank and tried to clean himself.

Joe came creeping out of the bushes. His eyes swelled up to the size of teacups when he saw Tough Guy. "You've been in swimming! Well!" he said. "Why did you go swimming?"

Tough Guy didn't answer for a minute. He was thinking. Then, "I just felt like swimming," he said. "Why don't you go in, too? The water's fine."

"Oh, no!" Joe said. "I—I just don't feel like it. I guess I've got a sort of a cold."

"I guess you're scared. I guess you're just a powder puff," said Tough Guy. He got up and shook himself. "I've done enough swimming for one day. I'm going home and clean up."

"What about the mouse?" Joe asked.

"Oh," said Tough Guy. "The mouse. Well, I couldn't be bothered. It was too small."

Tough Guy swaggered off. His tail dragged behind him wetly. He left Joe with his eyes popping
out, beside the pond.

He found his way out of the park. He darted
along the alley.

The stairs were easy now. Besides, Tough Guy
wasn't afraid of anything any more. He went up the
fire escape, paw over paw, as though he'd been
climbing stairs all his life.

He reached the ledge and he still swaggered boldly, dragging his wet tail behind him. He sat on the window sill, and dried himself in the sun. It had been a busy day. He was tired and he was very hungry but he was very happy. It would be a long, long time before Joe would call him "Powder Puff" again.

The next day was fine and warm. Tough Guy sat in the window. He gave himself a good bath, with his tiny red tongue. He hadn't liked his fuzzy gray self before. He had wanted a striped black and gray coat like Joe's. Now he liked his own. He knew now that the color of fur didn't matter. He was pretty sure, in his heart, that he wasn't a sissy.

Soon Joe appeared out of his own house across the way. Joe didn't look so tough. He tried to act tough, though. "Hi, there, Powder Puff," he started to sing out.

Tough Guy didn't give him a chance. HE sang out, "Well, well! Here's the powder puff. Well, Powder Puff, want to go swimming today?"

Joe made believe he didn't hear. He curled down, and shut his eyes.

Tough Guy finished washing behind his ears, and then he too settled down for a morning nap. He was just drowsing off when Joe, in a meek voice, called, "Tough Guy?"

"Yes?"

"Tough Guy, will you teach me to swim? I watched you swimming. You've got a nice stroke."

"Sure." Tough Guy shuddered to think of the cold water, but he wouldn't let Joe know that. "Sure, Joe. Any time."

He thought for a minute. Then he said, "Joe, will you teach me how to catch a mouse? I don't think I could have caught that one, even if I hadn't changed my mind and gone swimming yesterday instead. I think maybe I need a lesson in mouse catching. How about tomorrow?"

"All right, Tough Guy," said Joe. "Fine. To-morrow. It's a date."

5-710

236624

Bradbury
Tough Guy

DEMCO